U.S. Special Operations Forces

ELLEN HOPKINS

Heinemann Library
Chicago, Illinois

Designed by Herman Adler Design
Photo research by Bill Broyles
Printed in China by WKT Company Limited

08 07 06 05
10 9 8 7 6 5 4 3 2

Library of Congress Cataloging-in-Publication Data

Hopkins, Ellen.
   United States Special Operations Forces / by Ellen
Hopkins.
      p. cm. -- (U.S. Armed Forces)
Summary: Provides an overview of the United States Special
Forces, including their history, weapons, and vehicles.
Includes bibliographical references and index.
   ISBN 1-4034-0192-6 (Hardcover) -- ISBN 1-4034-0449-6
(Paperback)
   1. Special operations forces (Military science)--United
States--Juvenile literature. [1. Special operations forces
(Military science)] I. Title.
II. U.S. Armed Forces (Series).
   UA34.S64H67 2003
   356'.16--dc21

                              2002015487

Acknowledgments
The author and publisher are grateful to the following for
permission to reproduce copyright material:
Cover photograph by James A. Sugar/Corbis
Title page, pp. 15, 16L, 17, 23, 25, 28, 29T, 44 United States
Army; contents page, p. 14 One Mile High; p. 4 Scott
Nelson/Getty Images; pp. 5, 8, 9, 20, 29B, 32, 34, 35, 37,
39, 41 Department of Defense; p. 6 AFP/Corbis; p. 10 The
Granger Collection; pp. 11, 13, 16R, 18, 36, 38 Corbis; pp.
12, 19 Bettmann/Corbis; p. 21 Laffont Jean Pierre/Corbis
SYGMA; p. 22 Gary Kieffer/Zuma Press; p. 24 Scott Crisp;
pp. 26, 45 Wally Santana/AP Wide World Photos; p. 30
National Archives and Records Administration; p. 31 NASA
Langley Research Center; p. 33 Greg Mathieson/
MAI/TimePix; pp. 40, 42, 43 United States Marine Corps

Special thanks to Lt. Col. G.A. Lofaro for his review of
this book.

Every effort has been made to contact copyright holders
of any material reproduced in this book. Any omissions
will be rectified in subsequent printings if notice is given
to the publisher.

Note to the Reader: Some words are shown in
bold, **like this.** You can find out what they mean
by looking in the glossary.

Contents

Snake Eaters, Night Stalkers, and Seals

What's so special about Special Operations Forces (SOF)? These soldiers, sailors, airmen, and marine are specially trained to conduct and support special operations. Some are experts in **unconventional** or **guerrilla** warfare. Their **missions** include:

- search and rescue

- underwater searches

- locating targets on the ground that airplanes cannot find, such as underground **bunkers**

- direct action or small-scale strikes against an enemy

- organizing and training others to work within a country against an enemy

- giving **humanitarian** aid after natural or manmade disasters

- removing mines (Mines are small bombs, planted underground.)

- **counterdrug** activities

Most SOF people are called operators. Some are called snake eaters because they are so tough. One unit is nicknamed night stalkers. Another unit is the Navy's SEALS.

Special Operations soldiers often do unusual things to complete their missions. This may include riding the local horses to get around and blending in by not wearing a regular uniform.

Under U.S. law, only men can join SOF. To become an operator, a man must be in excellent physical condition. Most are airborne (parachute) and are also **SCUBA** qualified. Operators train in more than one skill. These include hand-to-hand **combat,** night fighting, and using special weapons.

Guerrilla is Spanish for "little war." Guerrilla warfare is carried out by individuals or small groups. They operate from hidden bases and often depend on local people for food, shelter, or information. Guerrillas move quickly to surprise the enemy. They will attack supply lines, ambush patrols, and cut communication lines. Their goal is to bother and weaken the enemy. Because they move quickly and can blend in with the local people, guerrillas are very hard to capture.

SOF go into any situation, no matter how dangerous it is. They often put their lives on the line to save the lives of others or fight the enemy. Right now, somewhere in the world, snake eaters, night stalkers, and SEALs are working to complete many types of missions.

This member of the U.S. Special Operations Forces gives a Bosnian child a comic book that warns about land mines.

Going In

In **conventional** war, armies meet head-to-head on battlefields. Often, the biggest army wins. Today, armies must be prepared to fight both conventional enemy forces and small groups of enemy soldiers who might hide among innocent people. Others may hide in caves and underground **bunkers.** Finding the enemy takes time and **technology.** Today's warfare involves special joint missions that use the skills of Air Force, Army, Navy, and Marine SOF. When the United States went to war with Afghanistan, all of the SOF units participated. Their mission was carried out in five stages.

Stage One

Piloted spy planes, such as the U-2 and RC-135, and **drones,** such as the Global Hawk, flew over Afghanistan. They picked up radio signals and

Modern technology helps get SOF onto the ground safely in enemy territory, but it does not always help them move into position to fight. In 2001 in Afghanistan, donkeys were the best way to travel. Tanks and trucks would have been too easy for the enemy to see.

recorded movements on the ground. They followed enemy forces and found targets.

Stage Two

United States Air Force (USAF) and Army helicopters dropped Green **Berets** behind enemy lines. These **elite** Army SOF performed ground **surveillance.** The Green Berets contacted Afghan forces called the Northern Alliance, who were already fighting the Taliban. The SOF and Northern Alliance worked together.

Stage Three

USAF AC-130 gunships protected Army Airborne Rangers as they parachuted into the region. They captured airfields. They also carried out hit-and-run raids on Taliban command centers. This crippled the enemy and destroyed its will to fight. With the help of the Northern Alliance forces, U.S. Army Special Forces units captured two cities from the enemy.

Stage Four

Small bands of enemy soldiers hid in the mountains near a city called Tora Bora. Now the United States sent in the Marine Corps Expeditionary Units along with units from the Army's 10th Mountain and 101st Airborne Divisions.

Over 46,000 active-duty and reserve **personnel** are members of U.S. Special Operations Forces units. These units include:
- The U.S. Army's Airborne Rangers, Special Forces (Green Berets) and Delta Force
- The U.S. Air Force's Pararescue (PJs) and Combat Control Teams (CCTs)
- The U.S. Navy's Sea, Air, and Land Teams (SEALS) and Special Boat Units

Stage Five

SOF searched the woods at Tora Bora and took prisoners of war. Others stood guard at the mountain passes to keep enemy soldiers from escaping.

SOF Weapons and Tactics

Each unit has certain **missions** that only it performs. But many units use the same weapons and **tactics**. Different units often train together. SOF soldiers train night and day, in all kinds of weather. Soldiers practice every **maneuver** over and over until they know what to do without having to think about it.

Land warfare training covers patrolling, river crossings, mountaineering, **ambush** techniques, and field **communications**. It also covers **demolitions**, weapons, and **marksmanship.**

Basic **SCUBA** training teaches diving, underwater **navigation**, and what to do if equipment fails.

Special Operations Forces using mortars.

Most SOF units are trained to use parachutes. They jump from jets high in the sky and from low-flying transport planes. Sometimes they freefall long distances straight down, fast and silent. Other times, they open their parachutes while still high in the sky for long, cross-country rides. **Operators** may even land in the water wearing full combat gear.

Helicopters are often used to deliver SOF. Sometimes they hover close to the ground so operators can jump off. Other times, operators balance on the **skids** and use a rope to lower themselves to the ground, about 100 feet (31 meters) below. This is called **rappelling.** One type of rappelling is known as fast roping. Soldiers slide down a thick rope, one right after the other. The method really is fast. An entire team can be on the ground in three to five seconds.

Special Operations Forces use many weapons.
- Mortars are small cannons.
- Grenades are small bombs, usually thrown by hand.
- Grenade launchers throw grenades farther than a person can.
- M-4 rifles are light and the handles fold down, making them easy to carry.
- Machine guns such as the M-240 and M-249 fire many bullets in rapid fire.
- M-9 pistols are used when targets are close.

Special Operations soldiers must be able to fast rope from a helicopter with as much as 50 pounds (23 kilograms) of equipment on their backs.

Rogers' Rangers, a Swamp Fox, and a Gray Ghost

The United States won independence from Britain in 1783. But one hundred years before then, special forces types of units patrolled this country (It would be many years before these soldiers were called SOF.). Fighting units called Rangers used **guerrilla tactics** as early as 1670. That was the time of the Pilgrims.

In the 1700s, a new group of Rangers was created by Major Robert Rogers. He hired about 1,500 **colonists.** They fought for the British. "Move fast and hit hard," was their **motto.** Rogers focused especially on security and tactics. It was the beginning of the Ranger tradition.

This picture from the 1800s shows Francis Marion leading his troops through a forest in South Carolina.

In 1775, the country got ready for the Revolutionary War against Britain. The colonial leaders decided that "six companies of expert riflemen be immediately raised in Pennsylvania, two in Maryland, and two in Virginia." These troops became the Corps of Rangers. Their hit-and-run strikes helped the Americans win the war. .

There were also Rangers in Connecticut, South Carolina, and Georgia. Rangers in the north, led

Know It

John Mosby was so hard to capture that he earned him the nickname the Gray Ghost. One time, with only nine men, Mosby defeated an entire Union **regiment.**

by Thomas Knowlton, were master spies. In the southern swamps, Francis Marion led daring guerrilla raids. Francis Marion was called the Swamp Fox because he was a master of surprise. His men were small in numbers, but they outsmarted the British and won many victories.

During the Civil War, Rangers fought for both sides. Confederate Colonel John Mosby was in charge of one group of Rangers. Mosby would surprise the Union forces and they would scatter. His spies would then locate targets to attack.

Mosby also protected southerners from Union soldiers. He created a model for **unconventional** warfare: weaken the enemy's **front line,** weaken its **infrastructure,** and win the support of the people.

20th-Century Rangers

The way that Rangers fought in wars changed during the 1900s. They took on more tasks and were better trained. During World War II, the United States Army used these **elite** units. They would surprise the enemy with quick attacks. Then they would move deeper into enemy territory. Their movements would confuse the enemy. These **tactics**, based on Robert Rodgers' ideas, remain the main model for today's military.

In 1950, during the Korean War, there was a search for volunteers who knew how to use parachutes. About 5,000 paratroopers, soldiers trained to use parachutes, applied for the "extremely hazardous duty." Those who were chosen formed the 1st Ranger Infantry Company (Airborne). Their training included **amphibious** operations, **low-altitude** night jumps, **demolitions,** **sabotage,** and close combat.

Know It

In World War II, the main Axis Powers were Germany, Italy, and Japan. Allied Forces included England, France, Canada, and the United States.

In the early morning of June 6, 1944, U.S. Rangers used rope ladders to fight their way up a cliff and destroy an enemy **artillery** position.

In the years after the Korean War, battles were fought in Vietnam, the Middle East, Grenada, Panama, Somalia, and Afghanistan. The Rangers went into battle by air, land, and water. They scouted, patrolled, raided, **ambushed,** and won back territory that had been lost to the enemy. Along the way, some were killed. They are heroes who gave their lives for their country.

Merrill's Marauders were under the command of Brigadier General Frank D. Merrill. Here, they patrol a jungle in Asia.

Elite Units of the Second World War

World War II elite units (they still were not officially called SOF, even though they performed special missions) from the United States included:

• Devil's Brigade soldiers, who fought in Italy and France. The unit's specialty was close combat against much larger forces.

• U.S. Army Rangers, who fought in North Africa, Sicily, Italy, Western Europe, and the Pacific. One unit, the Second Ranger Battalion, became famous for their part in the D-Day invasion of Normandy in France on June 6, 1944. Under heavy fire, they climbed cliffs to reach the enemy. Then, they destroyed enemy guns.

• Merrill's Marauders, who slogged through the jungles of Burma. They defeated the Japanese in 5 major battles and 30 smaller fights.

• Alamo Scouts led Rangers and Filipino guerrillas in an attack on a Japanese prison camp. They freed all 511 Allied soldiers who were in prison there.

Rangers Lead the Way

Today, the Rangers remain a key part of the United States military. One of the units is called the 75th Ranger **Regiment.** It is part of the United States Special Operations Command (USSOCOM). It is organized like this:

Know It

The words *section, platoon, company, headquarters, battalion,* and *regiment* are used to describe groups of military **personnel.** A section is the smallest group and a regiment is the biggest.

75th Ranger Regiment

1st Battalion, Hunter Army Airfield, Georgia

2nd Battalion, Fort Lewis, Washington

3rd Battalion, Fort Benning, Georgia

Each battalion has

One headquarters company, with up to 428 Rangers

Three rifle companies, with 152 Rangers in each

Each rifle company has

One headquarters company

Three rifle platoons

One weapons platoon

Each weapons platoon has

A mortar section, with two or three mortars

An antitank section, with three 3-man teams, firing antitank weapons

A **sniper** section with two 2-man sniper teams

The Ranger regiment has two main **missions.** One is to capture airfields and the other is to raid special targets. A usual mission would be to capture an enemy airfield. Larger combat forces that need to get into the area could then use the airfield. When other soldiers arrive, the Rangers can then go on **reconnaissance** or **ambush** missions. Rangers must move quickly because they carry only five days of supplies. Their weapons are light rifles or machine guns.

The Marine Corps is the only branch of the military that has chosen to keep command of its SOF. Army, Navy, and Air Force SOF are all under command of the U.S. Special Operations Command.

One Ranger battalion is picked to be Ready Reaction Force 1 (RRF1). That means the entire unit must be able to go to **combat** with only eighteen hours' notice. One of the rifle companies must be able to go with only nine hours' to get ready. The three battalions rotate RRF1 every thirteen weeks.

These Army Rangers are conducting a training exercise.

Earning the Ranger Tab

It is not easy to become a Ranger. Men from any branch of the armed services may apply for the program. The Ranger training course lasts 61 days. Training takes about twenty hours a day, seven days a week. Students must be in excellent shape. They must pass a medical exam, the Army Physical Fitness Test. They must also pass a **Combat** Water Survival Test.

Soldiers undergo very hard physical and mental challenges. Sometimes they must go hungry. Sometimes they must go without sleep. But they still must successfully plan and carry out Ranger-style operations during training exercises that seem like real war. Those who do well are rewarded with the Ranger tab.

A U.S. Ranger demonstrates **demolition** techniques to students.

When students graduate, they earn the Ranger tab.

This Ranger student is in mountaineer training.

Ranger training starts with the Benning Phase at Fort Benning, Georgia. It has two parts. The first part is advanced physical training. It includes running, marching, obstacle courses, swimming with fully-loaded backpacks, and hand-to-hand combat training. In the second part, soldiers learn air **assault,** patrolling, **communications,** and combat operations. Then they go through practice combat situations.

The Mountain Phase comes next. Soldiers learn basic mountain climbing, **rappelling,** and how to move through mountains. They do practice missions, using the skills they have learned. These missions are conducted day and night for eight days. They include being dropped into mountain territory, climbing steep slopes, cross-country marching, and crossing rivers.

The last phase is called the Florida Phase. It trains soldiers in small boat operations, stream crossing techniques, and jungle survival skills. Soldiers go through a fast-paced, twelve-day exercise, using **ambushes,** raids, and hand-to-hand combat skills.

Shadow Warriors

During World War II, a new kind unit to perform special missions was created by the Office of Strategic Services (OSS) in 1942. The men in it were called shadow warriors because they moved quickly and quietly through enemy territory.

In Europe, three-man teams parachuted behind enemy lines in France, Belgium, and Holland. The teams set up groups of people to fight against the enemy. They organized **guerrilla** operations against the Germans.

OSS shadow warriors also fought in Asia. In Burma, they organized 11,000 local tribesmen into a fighting force that killed 10,000 Japanese.

This member of the Special Forces updates information posted for the rest of his camp during World War II.

After World War II, the OSS broke up. Some people from its **intelligence** section moved to the new Central Intelligence Agency (CIA), which was formed in 1947. But two OSS members, Aaron Bank and Russell Volckmann, believed the army should keep a force of guerrilla-style fighters. In 1952, the U.S. Army

Know It

The Special Forces that were organized in 1952 became known as the Green **Berets.** But there were other Special Operations Forces that were formed first. The Rangers were the very first SOF. The Navy SEALS are also SOF.

Three members of the Kachin tribe work with a U.S. pilot in Burma in 1944. The man with the umbrella is protecting the pilot from the strong heat of the jungle sun. Some Kachin tribe members worked with the units conducting special missions.

created 2,300 slots for the new personnel. They were called Special Forces and later become known as the Green **Berets.**

Each man in this first special unit spoke at least two languages, held at least a sergeant's rank, and had airborne skills. The first SF unit was called the 10th Special Forces group. It began work on June 19, 1952 with ten soldiers. The unit was based at Fort Bragg in North Carolina.

By the end of 1952, the first Special Forces to operate behind enemy lines had been sent to Korea. The teams organized guerrillas known as fighters of liberty. Together, they conducted raids and rescued downed airmen. These early Special Forces missions remained secret for 30 years.

Within months, hundreds more men volunteered to join. Many had been Rangers, who operated openly in enemy territory. But they soon learned that this Special Forces unit might spend months deep within enemy territory. And they had to survive without help from the outside.

Green Berets

In 1961, President John F. Kennedy visited Fort Bragg. Kennedy was interested in **unconventional** warfare. He saw that these new Special Forces soldiers were the perfect men for the job. These men had been wearing green **berets** since 1953, to set themselves apart from other military units. With Kennedy's support, it became the official headgear for Army Special Forces soldiers, and they became know as the Green Berets.

Green Berets operate in A-Detachments, or A-Teams, that have twelve men. In Vietnam, they trained Vietnamese tribesmen in the skills of guerrilla warfare. But they also built schools and hospitals and gave medical care. This won them friends in Vietnam.

Before he went to Fort Bragg in 1961, President Kennedy sent word that all of the Army Special Forces soldiers should wear their green berets for his visit. He agreed that they deserved special attention for their work. In 1962, Kennedy wrote a memo calling the green beret "a symbol of excellence, a badge of courage, a mark of distinction in the fight for freedom." In his honor, Green Berets lay a wreath and green beret on his grave every November 22, the date of his assassination.

Army Special Forces are lifted out of a forest area by a special rope system attached to an MH-60G Pave Hawk. This system is used when there is no room for the helicopter to land.

Green Berets wade through a marsh to reach their target.

Today, the A-Team is still the basic Green Beret unit. Each Special Forces Company has six A-Teams. One of the six teams is trained in **combat** diving. Another is trained in free-fall parachuting. Each team has a captain. Sometimes the team splits into two six-man teams. The second in command is a warrant officer. The other ten members are noncommissioned officers (NCOs). All are **multilingual** and cross-trained in five areas. These are

Know It

Commissioned officers hold the rank of second lieutenant or above. Noncommissioned officers are lower ranked officers who have enlisted in the military. A warrant officer has a rank between the commissioned and the noncommissioned officers.

- weapons
- engineering and **demolitions**
- medicine
- **communications**
- operations and intelligence

To Free the Oppressed

Special Forces missions require special talents. Not every man can qualify. Before training even starts, every future Green **Beret** must complete the Special Forces Assessment and Selection (SFAS) program. This program is designed to put the men under physical and mental stress. The program lasts 24 days. Activities include

- physical fitness test
- swimming
- endurance runs and marches while carrying heavy knapsacks
- obstacle course
- land **navigation**
- basic first aid
- tying knots, **rappelling,** and log drills (a team of men carries a heavy log together)

This soldier may only be practicing, but the barbed wire he is squirming under is real.

Men who pass the SFAS move on to advanced training. The first part lasts 40 days. It covers land navigation, and small unit **tactics.** Then, the Green Berets are trained in their different areas of work. This training lasts from 24 weeks (weapons or engineering) to 57 weeks (medical training). Next comes 38 days of classes in **guerrilla** and airborne operations. Green Berets finish their training in language school at the Special Operations Academic Facility at Fort Bragg.

↑ This soldier is being trained on the "Nasty Nick" obstacle course.

Green Berets are trained to perform the following missions:

- **Unconventional** Warfare. This includes guerrilla warfare and organizing, training, and supplying local people so they can conduct guerrilla missions.

- Direct Action. Small-scale actions to take, damage, or destroy a target or recover **personnel.**

- Special **Reconnaissance.** SF teams go behind enemy lines to gather information about the enemy, the land, or the local people.

- Counter-terrorism. These measures are taken to prevent and respond to terrorism.

- **Psychological** Operations. These help convince people who live in other countries to support the United States.

These Special Forces soldiers are also taught to train and help the military forces of the countries they are living in. They are experts in their assigned country's native language and **culture.**

Walk With a Green Beret

Scott Crisp is a paramedic. A paramedic is someone trained in emergency medicine. Scott flies in a helicopter to reach accident victims. He also has a second job. Scott is an airborne medic for the Green **Berets.** As part of a twelve-man Special Forces A-Team, Scott says, "I'm first and foremost a member of a combat team. Then I'm a medic."

Scott joined the army when he finished high school. Since he was interested in skydiving, he later transferred to an Air Force Pararescue team.

In the air force, Scott learned about parachuting and doing military airborne operations. "We jump out of transport aircraft. We jump from helicopters. We even jump from jets. As you might guess, that's extremely dangerous." Scott says that SF train all the time.

Scott left the Air Force and joined the Army Reserves. That's when he decided to try out for the Green Berets. "I had many of the qualities they look for," he explains. "Parachute skills. Medical training. And I'm bilingual." Still, he had to pass the SFAS and advanced training. He started the selection process with 32 other men. Only Scott and one other man completed the training.

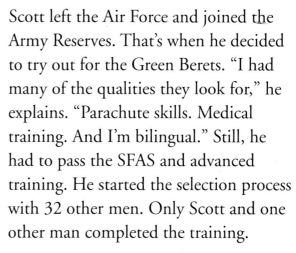

Scott Crisp drops safely from a helicopter (top) on his way to work! Scott, like all medics, must do his job wherever the soldiers are. So, medics dress like soldiers and even carry some of the same gear.

This member of the Special Forces is practicing a freefall from an airplane.

Scott is a reservist. He does not work for the Green Berets all the time. He works a few weekends every year for the 5th Special Forces Group. This group is based at Fort Campbell, Kentucky. "I could work every weekend if I wanted to. Most people don't realize Special Forces are at work, somewhere in the world, all the time. Because I speak Spanish, I am often [sent] to South and Central America. Most of our operations there are counterdrug [operations]."

Know It

Getting in and out of places is a tough part of Scott's job. To get in, an entire A-Team may go out of a helicopter on one line. To get back to the helicopter, they sometimes use a system called surface-to-air recovery. It is a balloon in a bomb casing. The casing blows open and the balloon inflates, lifting one or more soldiers into the air. A helicopter then snags them with a hook.

Top Secret Commandos

Imagine a group of SOF **commandos** whose **missions** are so secret that the U.S. government cannot even say they exist. There is such a group and they are the Delta Force. No one knows how many Delta Force **operators** there are, but we do know a few things about them.

In 1962, Colonel C. A. Beckwith worked with the British Special Air Service (SAS) commandos. When he returned to the United States, Beckwith started planning a new SOF unit. On November 19, 1977, the new 1st Special Forces Operational Detachment Delta was created. The British SAS was the model.

Army Special Forces move into position by the light of the moon in Afghanistan with local soldiers. However, these men are not Delta Force. The Delta Force is so secret that there are no pictures of them.

Delta Force operators specialize in **hostage** rescue, **reconnaissance**, and hand-to-hand combat. The men range in age from 25 to 40 but they can be older. They are considered to have the best **marksmanship** in the world. They carry the best and most modern weapons. Some are custom-made for the men who use them. Delta Force commandos are also trained to pick locks and use plastic explosives. They climb up and **rappel** from the sides of buildings and swim long distances in full gear. They also calm frightened hostages and provide medical care.

Delta commandos train in a large fenced area inside Fort Bragg. It is known as the Compound or the Ranch. Top Rangers and Green Berets may be invited to try out for the group. Only one in ten—the very best of the best—is chosen. Because the group's missions are secret, they cannot take credit for what they do. Often, even their families don't know what they do.

Delta Force missions

Sometimes Delta Force missions fail. One failed mission happened in 1980. Delta operators were sent to Iran to rescue a group of American hostages. But the rescue helicopter crashed. Since then, the new unit has taken part in U.S. military actions around the world:

- Before Operation Desert Storm began in 1991, Delta commandos were in Iraq, scouting missile positions.
- In 1993, four Deltas were killed with a group of Rangers in the streets of Mogadishu, Somalia.
- In the 1990s, Delta operators trained and guided Colombian police as they smashed a large cocaine-selling operation.
- In 1999, Deltas trained Pakistani commandos to go after Osama bin Laden, the leader of the group believed to have carried out the attacks on September 11, 2001.

Night Stalkers Don't Quit

In 1980, the U.S. Army decided to form a Special Operations Aviation Task Force to deliver SOF soldiers any time, anywhere, without fail. In 1982, the 160th Aviation Battalion was chosen for this job. The pilots and crews were all volunteers, known as Night Stalkers.

Their first official **mission** was in October, 1983. Comunists were trying to take over the island nation of Grenada in the Caribbean. The 160th got orders to take part in Operation Urgent Fury.

Six helicopters tried an air attack against a target. Under heavy enemy fire, the helicopters had to turn back. Their second try was a success, but all six helicopters were damaged. Then, two more helicopters were sent to protect the governor. As they approached his house, enemy soldiers began shooting. The helicopters escaped, then returned and put SOF on the ground to protect the governor. The 160th completed their mission and earned the motto, "Night Stalkers don't quit."

During Operation Desert Storm, Night Stalkers rescued an F-16 pilot at night 60 miles behind enemy lines. They also picked up a stranded Green **Beret** A-Team. The daylight mission was conducted by a single aircraft, in the middle of a firefight.

The MH-53J Pave Low IIIE is the largest and most powerful helicopter in the air force. It is also the most advanced in the world.

Pararescuemen practice climbing a moving rope ladder attached to a HH60-G Pave Hawk near Golden Gate bridge in California.

Two of the helicopters that crashed in Mogadishu, Somalia, during an operation in Africa, belonged to the 160th. When they went down, other Night Stalker pilots rushed to help their friends. One landed beside a downed helicopter in a narrow street. As the copilot pulled survivors from the wreckage, the pilot fired a gun from the cockpit. Under heavy gun fire, the rescue helicopter lifted off, with a survivor clinging to the **skids.** But five Night Stalkers lost their lives that day.

The 160th is considered the finest night fighting force in the world. They are the army's only SOF aviation force. Through much practice, Night Stalkers have developed night flight techniques and equipment that continue to be used.

The CH-47 Chinook helicopter is used by the U.S. Army.

That Others May Live

On December 21, 2001, a call came in to the U.S. Air Force's 56th Rescue **Squadron** based at Keflavik, Iceland. Strong rains and wind had created huge waves in the sea. A fishing boat had crashed against the rocks at the bottom of a tall cliff. The boat was sinking and a fisherman was clinging to the roof. Winds were gusting to 80 miles (129 kilometers) per hour. It was not a good day to fly helicopters, and it definitely was not safe to dangle beneath one. But that's exactly what this U.S. Air Force Pararescue team was about to do. Air Force parajumpers (PJs) are trained to rescue soldiers, astronauts, or civilians on land, in the sea, or in the air. PJs perform their **missions** "that others may live."

The helicopter took off even though it was very hard to see anything. The crew wore special night vision goggles. Ground teams shined spotlights over the cliff, and the pararescue team found the wrecked boat. Fighting wind and rain, the pilot got the helicopter into position. He struggled to hold it there while a PJ was lowered to the fisherman. The two were lifted to the waiting ground rescue team. Minutes later, giant waves swallowed the boat.

Loaded down with equipment, this PJ is ready to jump into the ocean. Note the fins on his feet.

The story of the PJs begins in 1943 during World War II. Over the jungle in Asia, 21 people had to jump from an airplane that was about to crash. A three-man rescue team volunteered to rescue them. The medics cared for the injured for a month while they led them to safety. Pararescue teams were also active during the Korean War. In Vietnam, the teams slid down rescue cables into the jungle. They picked up wounded soldiers and pilots whose planes had been shot down.

A step forward in pararescue combined parachuting with **SCUBA** diving. Before the space shuttle program was developed, spacecraft returning to Earth landed in the ocean. When the Gemini 8 space flight had mechanical problems, PJs flew to the splashdown site. They arrived just as the spacecraft hit the water. Three PJs parachuted into the ocean and attached floats to the craft. Then they stayed with astronauts until a navy rescue ship arrived three hours later.

Special Tactics Teams

There are six U.S. Air Force Special **Tactics Squadrons** that are made of **combat** controllers (CCTs) and pararescuemen. CCTs are sent in ahead of SOF to make an area safe for parachute or aircraft landings. Special tactics teams can also provide emergency medical treatment, rescue injured soldiers, and lead search-and-rescue missions.

During World War II, paratroopers sometimes landed 30 miles away from where they needed to be. Help from the ground could avoid these problems. So a company of airborne scouts was organized and trained. They would parachute into an area and guide inbound aircraft with lights and flares. Today's CCTs carry the best **communications** equipment. Each man usually carries about 100 pounds (45 kilograms) of gear.

Members of special tactics teams are trained in air traffic control, airborne skills, survival skills, and **SCUBA.** They also attend Combat Control school. CCTs have special communications skills. Using radios and satellites, they send information about the combat area to SOF on the ground, in aircraft, and even to officers back at headquarters.

An air combat controller sets up his maps, communications equipment, and binoculars. The winter weather does not stop him from his **mission.**

The 10th Combat Weather Squadron is trained to go into enemy territory and send back weather forecasts. This helps SOF know when they can fly their planes and drop paratroopers. These men are also trained in parachuting, survival skills, SCUBA, and mountain warfare.

How Special Tactics Teams get into position

Pararescuemen and CCTs are trained to enter an area in a number of ways:

From airplanes by
- parachuting from low-flying planes, with combat or SCUBA equipment; landings can be into water or forests
- parachuting from high-flying planes, using military freefall jumps
- parachuting from high-flying planes, using cross-country canopy flights

From the water by
- SCUBA or surface swimming
- dropping from an aircraft in a boat,
- using rubber raiding craft, which are inflatable rubber boats

From helicopters by
- **rappelling,** using a rope ladder, or a hoist

Through mountain operations by
- rock or ice climbing
- rappelling

Overland movement using
- motorcycles
- all-terrain vehicles, or regular motor vehicles

Arctic operations by
- skiing, or snowshoeing
- snowmobiling

The uniforms of these Special Operations Forces soldiers keep them warm and hide them in the snowy conditions. Note the white covers on their backpacks.

Riding the Pipeline

Climbing rock walls. **Rappelling** from a helicopter. Parachuting into choppy seas while wearing full **SCUBA** gear. These activities take nerves, hard training, and much practice. The training for pararescueman and **combat** controllers is called the pipeline. And it is as tough as it gets.

It begins with a Pararescue/Combat Control **Indoctrination** Course, or "indoc," that lasts ten weeks. Only one in ten will finish the course. Many hours are spent in the pool. Students have to swim while wearing belts with weights on them. They must tread water with their hands and feet tied. They also practice buddy breathing, in which two people share the same underwater air source.

Pararescue and combat controller students help each other finish after miles of marching in the Texas heat with 70-pound (32-kilogram) packs.

A U.S. Air Force senior airman moves across a concrete climbing wall during pararescue training. There are no safety ropes attached to him.

At the U.S. Army Special Operations Underwater School, students learn to SCUBA dive. They also learn to use a compass to **navigate**. They are taught how to sneak into enemy waters and what to do if their underwater equipment fails. Next comes underwater egress (*egress* means to go out) training at the Pensacola Naval Air Station. First, students are strapped into a dunker, which is a model of part of an airplane. Then they are dropped into cold water, and the dunker is flipped upside down. Students must quickly unbuckle themselves and swim out, as they would from a sinking aircraft.

Pipeline students learn basic parachute skills, how to freefall from high altitudes, how to set up and repack parachutes, and how to do night operations.

The last training that PJs and CCTs do together is the U.S. Air Force Survival School. This teaches students what to do their aircraft crashes or if they have to **eject** from their plane. One week is spent living off the land with a few simple tools and supplies.

Finally, pararescue students take combat medic courses. Then, they learn about weapons, mountain climbing, and saving downed airmen. Combat controllers take classes in air traffic control, **communications,** radar, **demolitions,** and field **tactics.**

Underwater Commandos

When the United States entered World War II, one thing became clear. Before navy ships could send sailors ashore, someone had to scout the beaches and clear obstacles like huge rocks. To meet this need, the navy formed its Naval Combat **Demolitions** Unit (NCDU). Their mission was dangerous because the beaches were guarded by enemy guns.

During World War II, plans were formed to invade the beaches at Normandy, in France. Thirty-four NCDUs were sent to clear the way. At Omaha beach, they were met with heavy enemy gunfire. Still, they managed to blow ten gaps in the German defenses. But 31 men were killed, and 60 were wounded.

In the Pacific ocean, some obstacles to the beaches were in the water. Many of the islands were surrounded by reefs that acted as natural obstacles. NCDUs became Underwater Demolition Teams (UDTs). The UDTs took part in every major Pacific landing.

UDTs also played important roles in the Korean War. Some cleared railroads, tunnels, and bridges along the Korean coast. Others found safe places for small boats to land. Still

Underwater demolition teams face dangers from the enemy and their own equipment. They must time their operations carefully.

SEAL Delivery Vehicle Teams get to their assignment by traveling underwater. They use submersibles, which are tiny submarines that fly through the water like airplanes. This model is powered by rechargeable batteries. It has a **communication** system that allows the men to talk to each other while underwater.

others located and marked underwater mines for special ships, called minesweepers, to destroy. And sometimes the UDTs went on rescue **missions.** In October, 1950, two minesweepers hit mines and sank. UDTs rescued 25 sailors.

In 1962, President Kennedy directed the military to create new units for **unconventional** warfare. The navy used UDT members for its new Sea, Land, and Air Teams, or SEALs. The SEAL mission was to conduct **guerrilla**-type operations in ocean or river environments.

In 1983, all remaining UDTs were reassigned to SEAL teams or SEAL Delivery Vehicle Teams.

By Sea, Land, and Air

The sea is cold and dark, especially at night. This is when most SEAL **missions** take place. Special suits keep divers dry but do not keep them warm. The cold water numbs fingers and toes. It can also affect how the brain works, making it hard to think. Darkness is a problem, too. It does help SEALs surprise the enemy. But it is hard for them to know where they are swimming.

Many things can go wrong underwater, so SEAL divers are always tied to a dive-buddy. During **combat** swims, one man holds the compass board. This has a compass, a watch, and a device called a depth gauge that tells them how deep they are. These things help keep the team on course. A dim light lets them read the board. They can see about six inches around them. The second diver holds his buddy's arm, serves as lookout, and counts kicks. To communicate, the divers use a code of squeezes and pauses.

A SEAL checks his compass board.

SEAL dive-buddies must work perfectly together. Over and over, they practice swimming 100 yards (91.5 meters), counting kicks. That tells them exactly how many kicks it takes to swim that far and how long it will take. Before they go on a mission, their route is planned. They know exactly how many kicks it will take to reach their target.

Many SEAL missions begin in the air. The same suits that keep divers dry underwater make them very hot in an airplane. The same fins that help divers swim make it hard for them to walk to the back of the plane and jump. The same parachutes that bring divers safely to the ocean can drown them in the water. As soon as a SEAL jumps from an aircraft, he begins to think about getting loose. By the time he hits the waves, he has freed himself from the parachute.

Many missions carry SEALS out of the water and beyond the beach. Like all SOF, they are well trained to fight on the ground in small units. Often, they work behind enemy lines in jungles or deserts or even in mountains.

Navy SEALS come ashore with their rifles.

The Few, The Proud

The U.S. Marine Corps (USMC) **motto** is "the few, the proud, the Marines." They are among the world's best **infantry** soldiers. The Marine Corps has smaller groups called Marine **Expeditionary** Units (MEUs). MEUs have more equipment and weapons than **conventional** Marine units. They are not really special operations forces. They are an example of a "special operations-capable" unit. The army's 82nd Airborne Division is another special operations-capable unit.

Marines from the 26th Marine Expeditionary Unit led a raid on a suspected terrorist camp near Kandahar, Afghanistan. Marines were based in Kandahar in support of Operation Enduring Freedom.

Marines from the 26th Marine Expeditionary Unit arrive at a beach in an inflatable Zodiac boat. This was part of an **amphibious** landing exercise.

There are seven MEUs. Three are stationed at Camp Pendleton in California. Three units are at Camp Lejeune in North Carolina. One is in Okinawa, Japan. Each unit has around 2,200 men and is organized like this:

- Ground **combat** element. It has a landing team that usually goes ashore first. It is followed by an **infantry** battalion that has waterborne and light armored vehicles and artillery.

- Aviation combat element. It has four types of helicopters. It also uses airplanes.

- Combat service support element. It has people who take of both equipment and **personnel.** It includes mechanics, engineers, doctors, and dentists.

- Command element. It has a commanding officer, who is a colonel, and his staff. It also has small groups called Maritime Special Purpose Forces.

Maritime Special Purpose Forces specialize in deep **reconnaissance,** hostage rescue, and **demolitions.** They often go in ahead of the MEUs. The MEUs provide **communications,** transportation, and supporting gunfire, if necessary.

A Force to Recon With

The Marine Corps is part of the navy and shares many things with other navy **personnel.** These include ships and aircraft. The Marine **Reconnaissance** Battalions, or Recon for short, began as World War II Raiders. In Korea, they worked with Underwater **Demolition** Teams on beach reconnaissance. They also destroyed tunnels and railroads that the enemy needed. Recon Marines also went deep behind enemy lines to gather information.

A Force Recon Marine steps off a helicopter and into the ocean. The Marines in the water are giving a "thumbs up" sign to say that they are okay after their jump.

After the Korean War, the Marine Recon troops learned new skills. They learned parachute skills and how to **SCUBA** dive They also earned inflatable boat skills. In 1957, the new Force Recon Marines were formed.

In Vietnam, small teams of Force Recon scouted the enemy. How did the North Vietnamese move? Where did they go? Moving quickly and quietly, Force Recon found the answers.

Force Recon Marines moved around in secret and stayed out of firefights. If they needed help, they called for backup.

Until 1998, there were two Marine reconnaissance units, Recon and Force Recon. Recon scouted beaches and landing locations for Marine operations. Force Recon went deep behind enemy lines to gather information. The two have been combined into one battalion. It is known as Force Recon.

Force Recon is divided into three sections, or companies. A Company trains new Recon Marines. The men learn the basic skills used by Force Recon battalions. After training, they move to B Company. There, they do patrolling in support of larger operations.

C Company is only for the most experienced Recon Marines. These are the SOF Marines that go deep into enemy territory for **surveillance**, underwater searches, prisoner snatches, **hostage** rescue, and to recover downed aircrews.

Force Recon Marines perform a Search and Seizure exercise.

The Future of Special Operations Forces

Today, the world's superpowers see the need for **diplomacy** rather than large-scale military actions. Most threats come from smaller countries and developing nations. Often the political situations there are unsettled. The United States military has shrunk by almost one-third since 1989, but there are three times as many SOF **missions**.

SOF will always be important. Satellites orbiting the earth can pick up radio and telephone signals. But that will not help if the enemy does not have telephones. Laser-guided bombs are very accurate. But who will tell the aircraft where to point their lasers.

Why SOF are so special

In April 1996, a civil war in Liberia, a country in Africa, forced Americans (and others) to the American Embassy. SEALS took up security positions as U.S. Air Force helicopters moved in. Over two weeks, the task force evacuated 2,126 people without ever firing a shot. It is that kind of discipline and training that makes SOF so valuable.

Even robots might help SOF complete missions in the future. This robot is used to investigate and remove explosive materials.

Terrorists often look just like the people they're hiding among. Someone who speaks the language and knows the culture must go and figure out who is who.

In the future, SOF will remain **combat**-ready. New technologies such as robotics, satellite **communications**, and computer-generated 3-D images will put them ahead of the enemy in any situation. But they will also continue to do peacetime missions such as disaster relief.

The United States Special Operations Forces are among the best in the world. The courage and dedication of these soldiers, sailors, and airmen makes them special. And they help make it possible to hope for a future free of terrorism and warfare.

Special Operations Forces continue to protect the United States by taking part in missions throughout the world.

Glossary

ally helper, supporter

ambush surprise attack

amphibious can operate on land and water

assault attack

beret soft, round cap made of wool.

bunker shelter that is partly or completely below ground

casualty member of the armed forces who has been killed or wounded

commando soldier that fights with unusual methods, such as hit-and-run

communication sharing information

conventional ordinary and traditional

culture the customs of certain people

demolition destroy something by blowing it up

diplomacy skillful handling of the relationship between nations

distinction special quality

elite the very best

front line place where most of the fighting takes place

hostage person who is captured and held against their will

humanitarian something that helps people

indoctrination teaching of basic ideas

infantry soldiers who fight on the ground

infrastructure bridges, toads, tunnels, buildings

low-altitude not too high in the sky

maneuver movement. Can also refer to a training exercise.

markmanship the skill to shoot at a target and nearly always hit it

multilingual speaks more than one language

navigation system to figure out where figuring out where a person is

operator member of a Special Operations Forces team

oppressed not treated kindly, often by a government

personnel persons employed by a branch of service

psychological refers to a how a person thinks

rappelling descending on a rope with short drops

reconnaissance gathering information by watching or studying

regiment military unit made up of several battalions

Resistance people who secretly fight for their freedom

sabotage destroy or damage buildings or equipment

SCUBA Self Contained Underwater Breathing Apparatus. This is the equipment used by divers.

sniper person in the military trained to shoot enemy soldiers from great distances

squadron type of military unit

surveillance watch kept over a person, place or thing

tactics methods of doing something

terrorism use of violence and fear to get something

trauma injury

unconventional unusual weapons or way of fighting

uprising revolt or rebellion

More Books to Read

Covert, Kim and Bob Holler. *U.S. Air Force Special Forces: Combat Controllers.* Mankato, Minn.: Capstone Press, 2000.

Covert, Kim and Bob Holler. *U.S. Air Force Special Forces: Pararescue.* Mankato, Minn.: Capstone Press, 2000.

Hamilton, John. *Armed Forces.* Edina, Minn.: ABDO, 2002.

Index